VISITING FEELINGS

Published by
MAGINATION PRESS
An Educational Publishing Foundation Book
American Psychological Association
750 First Street NE
Washington, DC 20002

For more information about our books, including a complete catalog, please write to us, call 1-800-374-2721, or visit our website at www.apa.org/pubs/magination.

Book design by Sandra Kimbell
Printed by Phoenix Color Corporation, Hagerstown, MD

Library of Congress Cataloging-in-Publication Data
Rubenstein, Lauren.
 Visiting feelings / by Lauren Rubenstein ; illustrated by Shelly Hehenberger.
    pages cm
 ISBN-13: 978-1-4338-1339-9 (hardcover)
 ISBN-10: 1-4338-1339-4 (hardcover)
 ISBN-13: 978-1-4338-1340-5 (pbk.)
 ISBN-10: 1-4338-1340-8 (pbk.)
 1. Emotions—Juvenile literature. I. Hehenberger, Shelly, illustrator II. Title.
 BF511.R793 2013
  152.4—dc23
                                        2013001222

First printing March 2013
Manufactured in the United States of America
10 9 8 7 6 5 4 3 2 1

VISITING FEELINGS

by Lauren Rubenstein, JD, PsyD
illustrated by Shelly Hehenberger

Magination Press • Washington, DC
American Psychological Association

Do you have a feeling
that's visiting today?

Can you open your door
and invite it to play?

Can you ask what it wants,
and then check it out?

Welcome it and listen to
what it's about?

What if the feeling plays hide-and-go-seek,
and won't let you see it, not even a peek?

Here's an idea, a good one to try:
Look at that feeling with wide-open eyes.

How does it look?
Is it short? Is it tall?

Is it thick or thin?
Or round like a ball?

Is it bright like the sun?
Dark like the rain?

Or is it a look you can't
even explain?

Now, how does it feel?

Is it light as a cloud, floating on air?
Or heavy and huge like a grizzly bear?

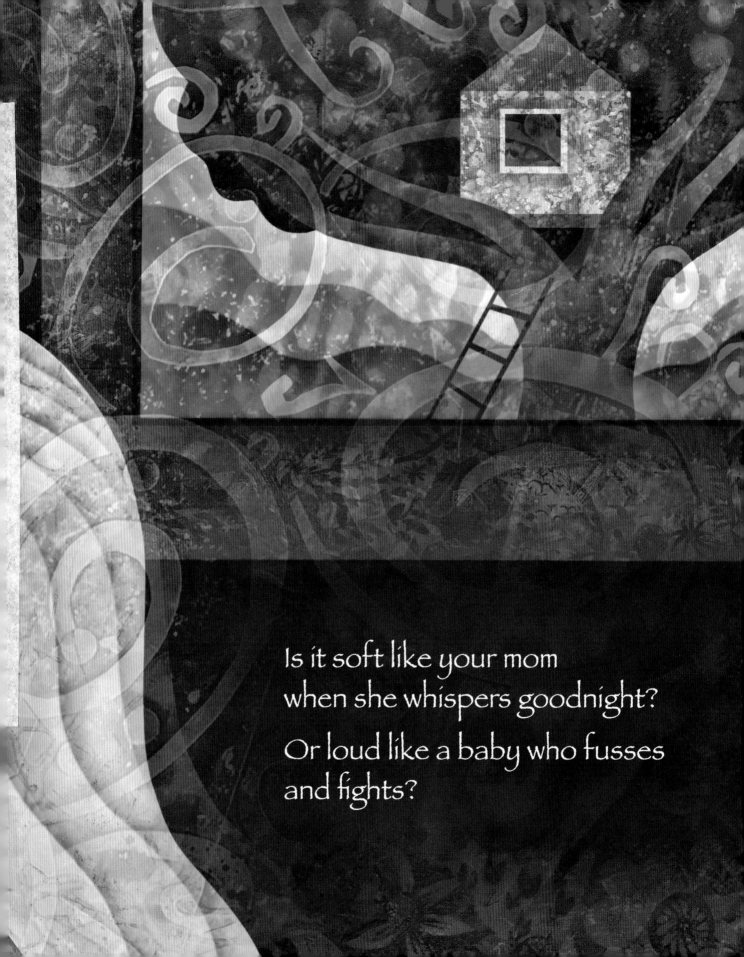

Is it soft like your mom
when she whispers goodnight?

Or loud like a baby who fusses
and fights?

Is it sharp like stepping
on stones with bare feet?

Or smooth like ice cream—
your favorite treat?

Is it warm or cold?
Sour or sweet?

Does it shiver with fear
when the two of you meet?

How did this feeling
enter your house?

Did it barge right in?
Was it shy like a mouse?

Did it rumble and grumble
like a thunderstorm blast?

Or was it quick as a
hummingbird darting
round fast?

And where has the feeling settled inside?

In your stomach, down low?
In your throat, up high?

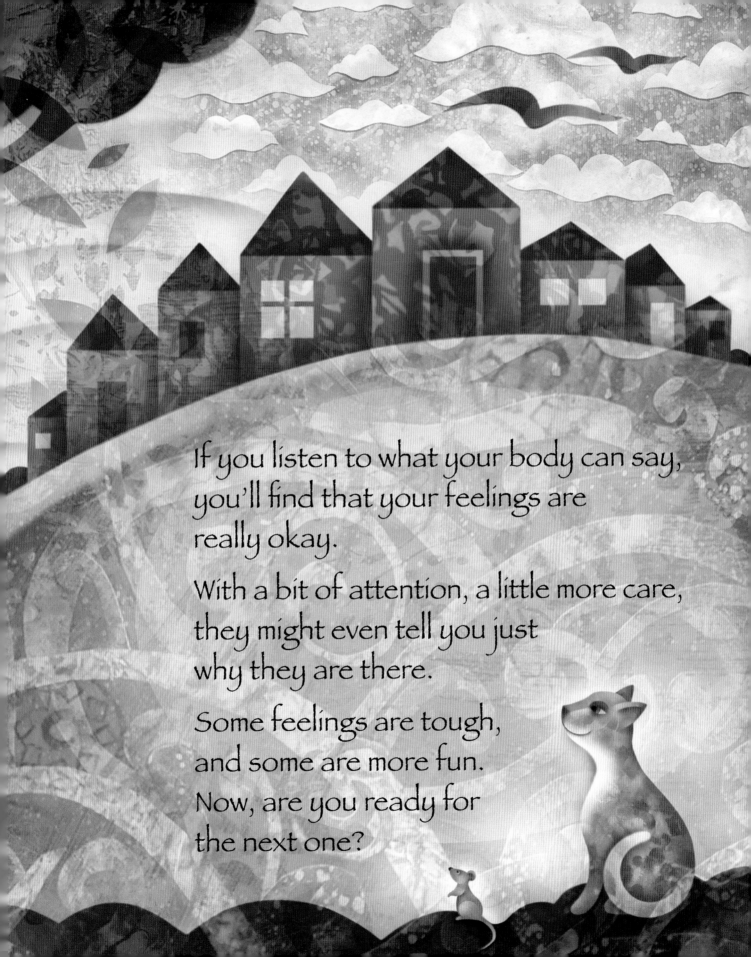

If you listen to what your body can say,
you'll find that your feelings are
really okay.

With a bit of attention, a little more care,
they might even tell you just
why they are there.

Some feelings are tough,
and some are more fun.
Now, are you ready for
the next one?

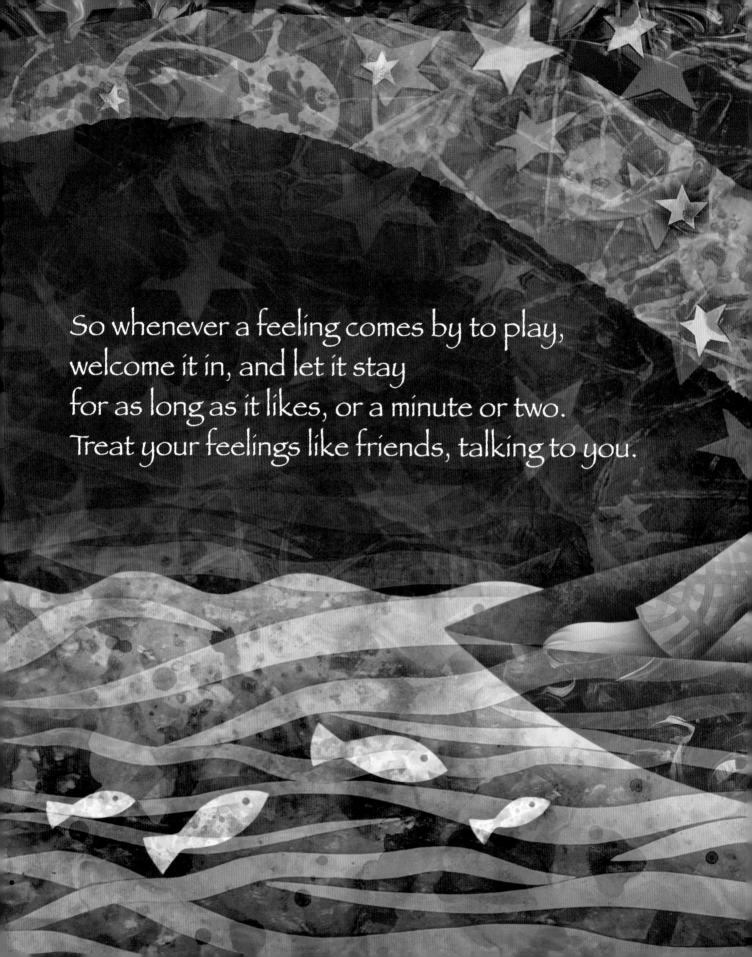

So whenever a feeling comes by to play,
welcome it in, and let it stay
for as long as it likes, or a minute or two.
Treat your feelings like friends, talking to you.

Note to Parents

Take a minute right now to pay attention to what's going on around you. What do you hear or see? Do you notice anything new? Now, turn your attention inward. What are you thinking and how do you feel?

Mindfulness—as you just experienced—is tuning into yourself and paying attention to the present moment without judging or analyzing what you are thinking or feeling. Although it seems quite simple, it is not easy. Our busy minds are constantly darting and drifting, telling stories about what has happened in the past and what might happen in the future.

Mindfulness is a powerful tool which can enhance many aspects of well-being. As parents, we can encourage our children to be mindful, to cultivate emotional intelligence through their senses, and to reflect on what they learn.

Linking Mindfulness and Emotions

Visiting Feelings harnesses the young child's innate capacity to fully experience the present moment. Rather than label or define specific emotions and feelings, *Visiting Feelings* invites children to sense, explore, and befriend all of their feelings with acceptance and equanimity. Emotions and feelings are neither good nor bad, acceptable nor unacceptable. Rather, they are simply present-moment experiences of felt sensations. This objectivity allows children to consider their emotions and gain a deeper understanding of themselves.

Visiting Feelings encourages children to treat their feelings like guests—welcome them in, get to know them, and perhaps learn why they are visiting. Feelings are treated as sensory experiences, with textures, colors, and sounds. Rather than suppress or try to undo feelings, it invites children to explore their feelings with their senses and even converse with them. Awareness of how feelings can lodge in the body, as conveyed by common expressions like "a pit in the stomach" or "a lump in the throat" is a form of emotional intelligence. This helps children handle any feelings that may arise with equanimity. It also helps children mindfully gain sensitivity to their bodies as rich kaleidoscopes of information. Children can cultivate this emotional intelligence through their senses by learning to explore the entire range of emotions they encounter within themselves on a daily basis.

Encouraging Mindfulness

Mindfulness can take many forms. Physical practice includes yoga, tai chi, martial arts, and even mindful walking. In fact, any activity can be done mindfully—for example, brushing your teeth, putting on your socks, or practicing the piano. There are many simple exercises you can do at home to help teach your child to be mindful.

Reflection activities can be introduced seamlessly into your family routine. Remember: "short times, many times" is ideal, both in terms of cultivating a mindful brain and fitting practice into busy schedules. For example:

- Before a family meal, have each person name three things they are grateful for. Discuss where the food came from and express gratitude for all those who helped along the way. Practicing gratitude provides a sense of meaning and connection, and increases one's overall sense of well-being.

- Try this well-known exercise. Hand your child a raisin, and ask that she use all five senses to explore the raisin before even putting it in her mouth. You can do the same. See how many adjectives you can come up with to describe the raisin's appearance, taste, touch, smell, and even sound (squish it close to your ear). You can try this with a bite-size portion of any food. For a fun variation, have everyone close their eyes and hand them something unknown to experience and describe.

Mindful breathing practices help regulate the nervous system, which kicks into fight-or-flight mode when we are stressed. Simple exercises can be done at home. Ask your children to watch a balloon expand and contract while counting inhales and exhales. Or place a small stuffed animal on your child's belly and ask him to "breathe" the animal to sleep. Here's another simple exercise borrowed from yoga practice that combines breathing with a visual cue:

1. Make a fist and breathe in through your nose. Have someone count to five out loud for you, or count it out in your mind.
2. Next, put up your hand with five fingers spread wide.
3. Breathe out through your nose. Exhale counting backwards from five, putting down one finger at a time with each count.
4. Repeat this pattern one to three times.

Cognitive exercises also encourage mindfulness. Reflection, insight, and empathy are essential skills which often take a backseat to academics in formal education. So to help develop these skills, try these exercises:

- Ask your child to tune in and count five sounds, five bodily sensations (e.g., warmth, tingling, pulsing), or five objects in the room that start with the letter "b." This is good practice for identifying but not acting on feelings and impulses that arise in the body.
- Encourage your child to change her own personal TV channel in her mind. When she practices switching back and forth from her favorite show, to something she doesn't like, to a neutral show, she is strengthening her ability to direct her attention.
- Similarly, ask your child to watch his thoughts like a parade passing. Ask him to notice whether the thoughts are big or small, loud or quiet, single or repetitive. His job is to keep watching the parade, rather than being swept into it—that is, caught up in his thoughts.

As newborns, we were more fully engaged in the world of the senses through voices, scents, colors, and of course, internal sensations of hunger. As we mature, however, verbal skills enable us to label our emotions, so that joy is often deemed "good," while anger or sadness is considered "bad." Motor skills enable us to flee from or act out our emotions. We have all witnessed this in a child's full-body temper tantrum. As our children become acculturated to our frenetic pace, they gradually forget how to simply be. Practicing mindfulness can help us return to the present.

Practicing mindfulness in childhood can help develop insight and empathy, or what Dr. Dan Siegel has termed "mindsight." Mindsight can actually transform the brain, creating new neural circuits and promoting reflection. Mindfulness can become a way of approaching life, fostering resilience and ultimately promoting well-being in the larger community. Experiencing mindfulness as a family is a remarkable gift for parents to give to their children. The emotional insight children gain will support them as they navigate their teen years and adulthood.

About the Author

Lauren Rubenstein, JD, PsyD, is a licensed clinical psychologist in private practice in Bethesda, MD. She also teaches yoga and mindfulness to children and adolescents, including kids in Haiti living in extreme poverty. Her humanitarian work in Haiti has been featured in the *Huffington Post*. Dr. Rubenstein plans to donate proceeds from *Visiting Feelings* to the Go Give Yoga Foundation.

About the Illustrator

Shelly Hehenberger studied art and design at Indiana University, and received her MFA in painting from the University of Cincinnati in 1994. Since that time she has worked as an art teacher, professional artist, and illustrator of children's books. The illustrations in this book were created digitally using hand-painted textures and overlays. She lives near Chapel Hill, NC, with her husband and 14-year-old daughter.

About Magination Press

Magination Press is an imprint of the American Psychological Association, the largest scientific and professional organization representing psychologists in the United States and the largest association of psychologists worldwide.